Phaeton and the Chariot of the Sun

by Nathan Patterson
illustrated by Rosiland Solomon

Orlando   Boston   Dallas   Chicago   San Diego

Visit *The Learning Site!*

www.harcourtschool.com

On a day long ago in Greece, a boy was walking to school. The boy's name was Phaeton. Phaeton was just like other boys except for one thing. Phaeton's father was the great Apollo.

The Greeks believed that Apollo moved the sun across the sky every day. He drove it in a chariot—a cart—pulled by strong horses.

On this day, two of Phaeton's classmates came up to him and asked, "Who do you say you are?"

"I am Phaeton!" he answered with pride. "My father, Apollo, drives the sun across the sky every day."

"What stories you make up!" said the other boys, who laughed and ran away.

Phaeton's feelings were hurt.

"I'll show them!" he said. He went to his mother. "I want to show everyone that my father is the one who drives the sun," he told her.

"How will you do that?" she asked.

"I want to visit him," Phaeton said.

"You may go," his mother said, "but be careful. It is a hard trip." As Phaeton left, his mother stood gazing after him.

Phaeton ran swiftly through forests. He waded across rivers. He traveled down deep canyons. Finally, he crossed one last canyon near the palace of Apollo. Soon he was gazing at bright golden walls and a roof made of gems. The palace glittered.

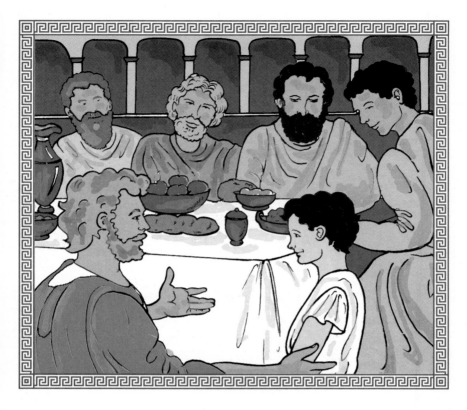

Inside the palace sat Apollo. Phaeton walked swiftly to his father's side. Apollo looked at him with pride.

"Welcome, son. I have arranged a feast for you. Whatever you want shall be yours," Apollo said. He was pleased that his son was brave enough to come and find him.

"There's only one thing I want," Phaeton said. "I wish to drive your chariot. I wish to drive the sun across the sky."

His father stepped back. "Oh, no, my son," he said. "I cannot allow that."

"It is the only thing I want," Phaeton said. He wondered if his father really drove the chariot at all.

Apollo was silent. At last he spoke. "I made a promise," he said, "and I will keep it. But I beg you to think again. It takes a skillful driver to control those strong horses. It is hard even for me."

"It is all I want," Phaeton said, and he crossed his arms. Apollo sighed. Then he arranged for Phaeton to drive the chariot.

"The first part of the path is very steep,"
Apollo told Phaeton. "The horses can
barely climb it. Hold on tightly, and steer
the horses well. You must be skillful to
move through the homes of the animals.
There is danger there. You will pass the
Lion, the Crab, and the Bull."

Apollo led his son to the chariot, which, like the palace, was made of gold and covered with jewels.

"Do not fly too high," Apollo warned. "If you do, you will burn up. Also, do not fly too low. That will set Earth on fire."

Phaeton nodded with excitement. He was going to drive the sun across the sky in his father's chariot!

"My son," Apollo said, "if there were any way to stop you, I would. But I have made a promise. So I ask you to be careful."

Phaeton started out. Before long, the horses could tell that the person driving them was not Apollo. They began to run this way and that. Soon they had pulled the chariot off the path the sun was to follow.

Phaeton could see that the sun was much too close to Earth. Right before his eyes, things on the ground were getting too hot. Trees caught fire. The ground dried up and cracked. Green grass became brown and then blew away, leaving only a sandy desert.

On Earth, the people begged for help.
"Apollo, help us!" they cried.

"Something is wrong!"

"The sun is too hot!"

"The sea is turning into steam!"

"The ground is too hot to walk on!"

Something had to be done. Zeus, who controlled lightning, climbed up to a high tower. He sent a bolt of lightning speeding toward the chariot. Thunder boomed, and rain poured from dark clouds. The rain cooled the ground and the seas.

The lightning hit the chariot, and it fell from the sky with Phaeton still in it.

Both Phaeton and the chariot tumbled to Earth. Phaeton fell into a river, where the water was already cool. Apollo swiftly used another chariot to catch the sun.

As Phaeton crawled out of the river, he thought of his pride. He was sorry he had ever asked to drive the sun across the sky. It was a very foolish thing to do. *Why did I not listen to my father, the great Apollo?* he wondered. Forever after, Phaeton would trust his father's advice.